The Secret Garden

Frances Hodgson Burnett

Simplified by Sue Ullstein
Illustrated by Annabel Large

Longman

Longman Group UK Limited,
Longman House, Burnt Mill, Harlow,
Essex CM20 2JE, England
and Associated Companies throughout the world.

This simplified edition © Longman Group UK Limited 1987

First published 1987

ISBN 0-582-54152-2

Set in 12/14 point Linotron 202 Versailles
Produced by Longman Group (FE) Limited
Printed in Hong Kong

Acknowledgements

The cover background is a wallpaper design called NUAGE,
courtesy of Osborne and Little plc.

Stage 2: 900 word vocabulary

Please look under *New words* at the back of this book
for explanations of words outside this stage.

Contents

Introduction

Frances Hodgson Burnett

Frances Hodgson was born in Manchester, England, in 1849. Her father was successful as a dealer in metal goods, but he died while Frances was still very young. The family continued to deal in metal goods, but more and more of their trade was with the southern states of America. The American Civil War, between the northern states and some southern states (1861–65), ended badly for the southern states and for the Hodgson company. The Hodgsons went to the United States and lived in the state of Tennessee.

They were very poor until Frances had some success as a writer from 1866, when she was seventeen years old.

In 1873, Frances Hodgson married Dr Swan Burnett. Her name was already known to many readers, so Mrs Frances Burnett kept the "Hodgson" in her name as a writer.

She had great success with her novel *Little Lord Fauntleroy* in 1886. Learned people now think that this story of an American boy who becomes an English lord is not good because it plays too much on the reader's feelings. But thousands of people enjoyed it.

The Secret Garden came out in 1909. It was written for children, but older people enjoy it because it shows the writer's surprising understanding of children, even when she herself was sixty years old.

Frances Hodgson Burnett died in 1924 in Long Island, USA.

The Secret Garden

The story begins in India at a time when very many British people lived there. They worked in government, in the army, on the railways and in trade. They were not all like the father and mother of Mary in this story, but many of them had plenty of Indian servants, and sometimes the European mothers did not give enough time and care to their own children. The hot season was not good for Europeans, and there were illnesses that the doctors did not know much about. That is how Mary became an unhealthy, rather nasty child.

England would seem a strange country after the India that Mary knew. And the Yorkshire moors would be even stranger. They are cold in winter. The wind blows strongly over them, with very few trees to stop it. You don't see many houses on the high moors, and the rough grass is all right for sheep but not for cows or other farm animals. The Yorkshire people believe it is very healthy, but an unhappy little child from India wouldn't think so at first.

Misselthwaite Manor and the moor

Chapter 1
There is no one left

Mary Lennox was born in India. Her mother and father were from England, but they lived in India because her father worked there. Mary's mother was very beautiful. She had many friends and she liked to go out with them. She was always with her friends. She had not really wanted a child at all. Mary's father was often out, too, because he worked very hard. So Mary did not see her mother or father very often. Servants took care of her. They did everything to please her and to stop her crying.

Mary was a thin, ugly baby who was often ill. She did not get better as she grew bigger. She was always a thin, unhealthy child. Because the servants always did what she wanted, she was not at all a nice child. She thought only about herself. No one loved Mary, and Mary loved no one.

One very hot morning when Mary was nine years old, a new servant came to wake her. Mary was cross because she wanted the servant whom she knew, not a new one.

The woman looked frightened, but Mary's own servant did not come. Later, Mary was left alone. It was a strange morning. No one told her what to do, so she went into the garden to play. She played with flowers and made a little garden of her own. She was cross because she did not know why she was alone. Something was not right.

Later she heard her mother talking and then she knew what was not right. Many people in the house were ill, and some had died. No one thought about Mary. No one wanted her, and she was sad. She was frightened, too. She went to her room. She cried and then she slept for a long time. When she woke up, the house was very quiet.

"Perhaps the sickness has gone," she thought. "Perhaps everyone is better. Now someone will come and look for me."

But no one came. She waited, but the house was still very quiet. Suddenly she heard footsteps outside her room, and two men came in.

"Barney!" the first man cried. "There's a child in here! A child alone! In a place like this! Who is she?"

"I am Mary Lennox," the little girl said crossly. "I went to sleep when everyone was ill, and I have just woken up. Why does no one come? Why didn't they remember me?"

"Poor little girl!" said the man called Barney. "There is no one left who could remember you."

And so Mary learnt that her father and mother were dead. The servants had all run away, and no one thought about the little girl who was left alone in the house. She was not a nice child, and no one cared about her.

Chapter 2
Mary goes to England

Mary had no family in India, so she went home to England to live with her uncle, Mr Archibald Craven. Mary had never been to England and she knew nothing about her uncle, who was her mother's brother. She was told that he lived in a big old house in the country, and that he was a hunchback. This frightened Mary. She thought, too, about Yorkshire, and the place where she was going to live. She knew only that it was called Misselthwaite Manor, and that Yorkshire was in the north of England.

One of Mr Craven's servants, Mrs Medlock, met Mary in London. She was a fat woman with a red face and little black eyes. Mary did not like her at all, and Mrs Medlock did not seem to like Mary very much.

During the journey to Yorkshire by train, Mary sat silently and looked out of the window. She had nothing to read, and she looked ugly and cross. Her black dress made her look colourless and ill. Since her mother and father's death she had begun to think strange thoughts. She had begun to wonder why she always felt so alone. Other children seemed to be part of a family with their mothers and fathers; but even when her mother and father were alive, she had never seemed to be part of a family. She had had food and clothes and servants to take care of her, but no one had really loved her. She did not know that this was because she was not a nice child. She did not know that she was not nice.

Mrs Medlock had never seen a child who sat so still and did nothing. Mrs Medlock did not like sitting quietly, so at last she said to Mary: "Do you know your uncle?"

"No," answered Mary.

"Didn't your father and mother talk about him?"

"No," said Mary again. Her father and mother had never talked to her about anything.

"Oh," said Mrs Medlock, and she was silent. Then she began again: "Do you know that you're going to a very strange place?" she asked.

Mary did not answer, and Mrs Medlock was surprised because the child was not interested in where she was going to live.

"The house is six hundred years old, and it's near the moor," she went on. "There are a hundred rooms, but most of them are shut up and are not used. There are big gardens round the house, and trees, and ..." she stopped and then she said, "But there's nothing more."

Mary was always interested in new things, but she did not want people to know that she was interested, so she sat still.

"Well," said Mrs Medlock. "What do you think of it?"

"Nothing," Mary answered.

This made Mrs Medlock laugh. "Eh!" she said. "You're like a little old woman. Don't you care?"

"It isn't important whether I care or not," said Mary.

"You're right," said Mrs Medlock. "It isn't important. I don't know why you're coming to Misselthwaite Manor, but I'm sure that Mr Craven isn't going to take any notice of you. He never takes any notice of anyone. He's a strange man, and he's a hunchback. He was never happy until he was married."

Mary looked at Mrs Medlock carefully. She was surprised to think of a hunchback being married. Mrs Medlock was pleased that at last the child seemed to be interested in something.

"His wife was a sweet, pretty woman," she said. "He loved her more than anything in the world. When she died——"

"Oh! Did she die?" Mary asked. Suddenly she felt sorry for Mr Craven.

"Yes, she died," Mrs Medlock answered. "And now he's as strange as ever. He's away most of the time; and when he is at Misselthwaite Manor, he stays in one part of the house and only his servant sees him."

It sounded like a story from a book, and it made Mary feel sad: a house with a hundred rooms – near a moor (and Mary did not know what a moor was) – a man who was a hunchback and who did not like people.

Chapter 3
Across the moor

Mary slept for a long time. It was dark when she woke up.

"Wake up!" cried Mrs Medlock. "This is where we get out. Quickly! We've still got a long drive to the manor."

It was still raining. Mary was wide awake now. She wanted to see the strange place which Mrs Medlock had told her about.

"What is a moor?" she asked suddenly.

"Look out of the window in ten minutes time and you'll see it," Mrs Medlock answered. "We have to drive five miles across the moor, but you won't see much because it's a dark night."

Mary did not ask any more questions. She sat and looked out of the window. First, they drove through a small town, and then they were out in the open country, where there were only trees and fields. Then the horses began to climb up a hill. There were no trees or fields now. Mary could see very little in the darkness.

"We're on the moor now," said Mrs Medlock.

The wind made a strange, low sound.

"It's ... it's not the sea, is it?" asked Mary.

"No, it's not," answered Mrs Medlock. "It isn't the sea and it isn't fields, nor is it mountains. It's just miles and miles of land where nothing grows except rough grass."

"It sounds like the sea now," said Mary.

"That's because of the wind," said Mrs Medlock. "It's a sad place, I think, but some people like it. It's very pretty in the spring when the flowers are out."

On and on they drove through the darkness. The road went up and down, and Mary felt that the journey would never end.

"I don't like it," she said. "I don't like it."

At last they stopped in front of a long, low house. Mary could see only one light in the whole house. Inside, she found herself in a large, dark room. She looked very small in her black coat, and she felt very small, too. Then Mrs Medlock took her to her room. They walked for a long time. At last Mrs Medlock said: "Well, here you are! This room and the next one are yours – and you must stay in them. Remember that!"

And so Mary began her life at Misselthwaite Manor, and she had never felt so cross and alone in her life. She was also rather frightened.

Chapter 4
Martha

Mary woke up the next morning when one of the servants came into her room. Outside the window she could see miles and miles of land, that looked like an endless red-blue sea. There were no trees.

"What is that?" she asked the servant.

"That's the moor," said the girl, and she smiled kindly. "Do you like it?"

"No," said Mary. "I hate it."

"That's because you don't know it," the servant girl answered. "I love it. It's very beautiful in the spring and summer when the flowers are out. The air smells fresh and the sky is blue and the birds sing."

This servant, whose name was Martha, surprised Mary. She was not like the servants in India, who spoke only when she spoke to them, and who always did what she wanted.

"You are a strange servant," she said.

Martha looked at Mary, who was still in bed, and laughed. She seemed to be a kind person; she had a round, healthy face, and she laughed a great deal.

"Are you going to be my servant?" Mary asked.

"I'll help you a bit, but you won't need me much," Martha said.

"Who's going to dress me?" Mary went on.

Martha looked surprised. "Can't you put your clothes on yourself?" she asked.

"No," said Mary crossly. "I've never dressed myself in my life."

"Well," said Martha, "you must learn now."

Mary was very angry now. She did not like this servant who would not help her. And suddenly she felt all alone. She did not understand Martha and Martha did not understand her. She started to cry quietly.

Martha felt sorry for the child. She went over to the bed and said kindly: "Eh! You mustn't cry like that. You mustn't. Come, it's time to get up now. I'll help you to get dressed."

Martha's voice was so kind that Mary stopped crying. She got out of bed, and Martha brought her clothes. They were not the clothes which she had had on the journey. They were new.

"Those aren't mine," Mary said. "Mine are black." She looked at the white dress and coat and added, "Those are nicer than mine."

"Mr Craven doesn't want you to have black clothes," said Martha.

"I hate black things," said Mary.

While Mary put on her clothes, Martha talked.

"There are twelve of us," she said. "And my father was very little money. So it's hard for my mother to find enough food. But the children play on the moor, and mother says that the fresh air makes them healthy, like the little wild horses which live there. My brother Dickon, who's twelve years old, has a horse."

"Where did he get it?" Mary asked.

"He found it on the moor when it was a baby, and he made friends with it. Now the little horse follows him everywhere, and he rides on its back. Dickon is a kind boy, and animals like him."

Mary had always wanted an animal of her own and she began to be interested in Dickon. This was perhaps the first time she had ever been interested in anyone except herself.

Then she and Martha went into the next room, where a meal was waiting. Mary had never been a hungry child, and she did not want to eat now.

"I don't want any food," she said.

"But it's very good," said Martha, who was surprised. "If my brothers and sisters were here, there wouldn't be any food on that table in five minutes time."

"Why?" asked Mary coldly.

"Because they've never had enough food in their lives. They're always hungry."

"I've never been hungry, so I don't know what it's like," Mary said.

"Well," said Martha, "perhaps you ought to try it!"

"Why don't you take the food to your family?" Mary said.

"It's not mine," said Martha crossly. "And I

can't go home today. I have to work. I can only go home once a month."

At last Mary ate a little food.

"Now go outside and play in the gardens," said Martha. "Perhaps you'll want your food after you've been in the fresh air."

Mary went to the window. It was winter, and it looked very cold outside.

"It's too cold," she said.

"Well, if you don't go outside, you'll have to stay here, and there's nothing for you to do here," Martha answered.

Mary looked around. It was true. Perhaps she would go outside and see the gardens.

"Who will go with me?" she asked.

"No one," said Martha. "You must learn to play alone. Dickon goes out on to the moor alone."

When Mary heard about Dickon, she thought that she would go out into the gardens. Martha showed her the way.

"If you go round that way," she said, "you'll come to the gardens." She stopped and then she went on: "One of the gardens is shut up. No one has been inside it for ten years."

"Why?" asked Mary, interested again.

"Mr Craven shut it ten years ago, when his wife died. He won't let anyone go into it. It was his wife's garden. He shut the door and hid the key. But I must go now. Mrs Medlock wants me."

Chapter 5
Ben Weatherstaff and the robin

After Martha had gone, Mary went into the gardens. She was thinking about the garden that no one had been into for ten years. She wondered what it looked like. She wanted very much to see it. Why had Mr Craven shut it up and hidden the key? He had loved his wife, so why did he hate her garden? She wanted to see Mr Craven, but she knew he would not like her.

"People never like me, and I never like people," she thought.

The garden she was in now was certainly not the one which was shut up. She did not think this garden was very pretty, because there was nothing growing in it – only a few trees.

Mary walked through a door into another garden, which was the same as the first one. There was a high wall in front of her at the end of this second garden. She looked for a door in the wall, but she could not find one. She did not think that the gardens ended there, because she could see trees above the wall.

She was still thinking about the secret garden when she saw a little bird with some bright red feathers sitting in one of the trees on the other side of the wall. Suddenly he started to sing – it almost seemed that he was calling to her. His singing made her feel very happy. She was feeling all alone and the little bird made her feel much better. She almost laughed. She liked him.

"Perhaps he lives in the secret garden, and knows all about it," she thought.

She walked back into the first garden and found an old man there. He was working. His face looked cross, and he did not seem to be pleased to see her. But then she did not seem to be pleased to see him.

"What is this place?" she asked him.

"One of the kitchen gardens," he answered crossly.

"And what is that?" she asked, and she looked through the door into the second garden.

"Another kitchen garden," he answered, more crossly this time.

"Can I go into the last garden?" she went on.

The old man stopped working. "Which garden?" he asked quickly.

"The one with the high wall," Mary answered quietly. "There were trees on the other side of the wall, and I saw a little bird with red feathers in one of them. He was singing."

To her surprise, the old man suddenly laughed. His face changed, and Mary thought how much nicer a person looks when he laughs.

The old man turned towards the little bird's garden, and began to make a soft, kind sound. Then a wonderful thing happened. The little bird flew down and stood on the ground near the old man's foot.

"Where have you been, little one?" the old man asked quietly. He spoke to the little bird as if it were a child. "I haven't seen you at all today."

The little bird put his head on one side and looked at the old man. He was so pretty and he made Mary feel happy.

"Does he always come when you make that sound?" she asked.

"Yes, he does."

"What is he?" she asked.

"Don't you know? He's a robin. They're very friendly little birds. He knows that we're talking about him now. He likes to hear people talk about him." And the old man laughed. He seemed to like the little robin very much.

He went on: "When he was a baby, his mother died. He was all alone."

Mary felt strange when she heard this. She went nearer the robin, and said quietly: "I'm all alone, too."

The old man looked at her. "Are you the little girl from India?" he asked.

"Yes," answered Mary.

"Then I'm sure that you're all alone," he said.

"What's your name?" Mary asked him.

"Ben Weatherstaff," he answered, and he laughed. "I'm all alone, too, but not when the robin's with me. He's my only friend."

"I have no friends," said Mary. "I've never had any. I've never played with anyone."

"You and I are the same," Ben went on. "We

don't look nice and friendly, and I don't think that we are!"

Mary had never heard the truth about herself before. She wondered if she usually looked as cross and unkind as Ben Weatherstaff.

Suddenly the robin began to sing.

"Why is he doing that?" she asked.

"He wants to be your friend," the old man answered.

"My friend?" she asked. "Do you really want to be my friend?" she asked the robin as if she were talking to a person. Her voice was soft and kind, and Ben Weatherstaff was surprised.

"Why," he cried, "you said that very nicely. Perhaps you are a real child and not a cross old woman. You sounded just like Dickon then."

"Do you know Dickon?" Mary asked.

"Of course I do. Everyone knows Dickon Sowerby."

Mary wanted to ask Ben Weatherstaff more questions about Dickon and the robin, but suddenly the robin flew away.

"He was flown over the wall," said Mary. "He has flown into the garden which hasn't a door. I want to see that garden so much. There must be a door."

"There was a door ten years ago, but there isn't one now, and that's that," Ben answered, and he sounded cross again. "Now go away. I must work." And quite suddenly, he walked away.

Chapter 6
The cry in the passage

At the beginning of Mary's stay at Misselthwaite Manor, every day was the same. Each morning when she woke up Martha was lighting the fire, and a meal was waiting in the next room. Later she went outside into the gardens because there was nothing to do inside the house. Although Mary did not know it, this was the best thing for her.

One morning when she woke up, she felt hungry. At last she knew what it felt like. To her surprise, she ate all her food.

"It's good today," she said to Martha.

"You're hungry because of the fresh air from the moor," Martha said. "Soon you'll be really healthy."

"But I have nothing to play with in the gardens," said Mary.

"Nothing to play with!" cried Martha. "My brothers and sisters play with whatever they can find. They just run about and look at things."

And that is what Mary did.

She went to one part of the gardens more than any other: to the place where she had first seen the robin. A lot of dark green plants grew there by the wall. One day Mary was wondering why there were so many plants there when suddenly she heard the robin singing. He was sitting on the top of the wall, and he looked down at her, with his little head on one side.

"Oh!" cried Mary. "Is it you – is it you?" She spoke to him as if he were a person who could answer her. And he did answer her – he sang. Mary felt that she knew what he was saying: "Good morning! Isn't the wind nice? Isn't the sun nice? Isn't everything nice? Come on! Come on!"

And Mary began to laugh. "I like you! I like you!" she cried and she tried to sing, too. He flew away suddenly and sat in a tree on the other side of the wall. Mary remembered that the tree was in the secret garden. She wished that she could fly over the wall and see the garden.

Mary stayed outside all day, and she thought about the garden a great deal. That evening, when she sat down to eat, she felt hungry and tired, but she did not mind when Martha started to talk. After dinner, she sat in front of the fire, and Martha sat down beside her. At last Mary asked a question which she had wanted to ask for a long time.

"Why does Mr Craven hate the garden?"

"Are you still thinking about that garden?" Martha asked. "I knew you would. I was the same when I first heard about it."

"But why does he hate it?" Mary asked again.

At first Martha did not answer, but then she told Mary everything she knew.

"Now remember this," she began, "Mrs Medlock said that we mustn't talk about it; so don't

17

tell anyone that I told you."

Mary said that she would not tell, so Martha went on: "It was Mrs Craven's garden. She made it when they were first married, and she loved it very much. She and Mr Craven took care of it themselves, and the gardeners never went into it. There was a tree in the garden where Mrs Craven used to sit. One day part of the tree broke and she fell. She was very badly hurt, and the next day she died. Mr Craven was so sad that the doctors thought he would die too, but he didn't. He has been sad ever since, poor man. There – now you know why he hates the garden and never goes into it."

Mary did not ask any more questions. She felt very sorry for Mr Craven. Outside on the moor the wind was making a noise, and Mary was glad that she was inside the house. Suddenly, she heard another noise. It sounded almost the same as the wind, but it was inside the house. It sounded like a child crying far away.

"Can you hear someone crying?" she said.

"No," Martha answered quickly. "It's only the wind."

Then the crying came again, and somewhere in the house a door closed.

"There!" said Mary. "Someone *is* crying. I told you so! And it's a child."

This time Martha answered crossly. "It was the wind or one of the servants who has had a headache all day."

Chapter 7
"There was someone crying – there was!"

The next day it was raining, and Mary could not see the moor outside the window.

"What am I going to do today?" she asked Martha. "I can't go out into the gardens and there is nothing to do here."

"Can you read?" Martha asked.

"Yes," answered Mary.

"Well, why don't you read?" Martha said.

"I haven't any books," Mary answered.

"Perhaps Mrs Medlock will let you go into the room where Mr Craven keeps his books," Martha went on.

But Mary did not ask where this room was. She wanted to find it by herself. And so, after Martha had gone, she opened the door of her room, and went into the passage to look for Mr Craven's books. She did not really mind whether she found the room or not, but Mrs Medlock had told her about the hundred rooms during the train journey, and Mary wanted to see inside some of them.

Mary walked a long way that morning. There were many passages in the house, and many, many doors. She felt very strange as she walked past them. At last, on the second floor, she opened one of the doors. Inside was a big bedroom. After that, she opened more and more doors, until she began to think that she had been into every room in the house.

She lost her way two or three times when she tried to find her own room again. At last she reached her own floor, but she still could not find her own room.

"How quiet it is!" she thought.

Just then, however, she heard a sound – the same sound that she had heard the night before.

"It's nearer than it was last night," she thought.

Suddenly a door opened, and there was Mrs Medlock. She was very angry when she saw Mary.

"What are you doing here?" she shouted. "Didn't I tell you to stay in your own room?"

"I made a mistake," Mary answered. "I thought I heard someone crying." She really hated Mrs Medlock now.

"Of course you didn't hear anyone crying," Mrs Medlock said. "Go back to your room at once, or I'll hit you hard." And she pulled Mary along the passage to her room.

"Now stay there," she said. "Mr Craven was right. You need a teacher. I've no time to take care of a child."

When she had gone, Mary sat down in front of the fire. She did not cry, but she was very angry and sad at the same time.

"There was someone crying – there was – there was!"

Chapter 8
The key of the garden

Two days later, when Mary woke up in the morning, she sat up in bed and called to Martha: "Look, the sun is shining!"

"Yes," said Martha. "Spring is coming."

"I thought it always rained in England," said Mary.

"Oh no, of course it doesn't," laughed Martha. "Yorkshire's the sunniest place on earth sometimes."

"I'd like to see your house very much," said Mary.

"I'll ask my mother," said Martha. "I don't have to work today, so I'm going home."

"I like your mother," Mary said, "although I've never met her. And I like Dickon, too, although I've never met him."

"I wonder what Dickon would think of you?" Martha said.

"He wouldn't like me," said Mary. "No one ever does."

Martha looked thoughtful, and then she said: "But do you like yourself, Mary?"

Mary thought, and then she answered: "Well . . . no, not really – but I've never thought of that before."

Martha laughed. "Mother said that to me once, when I was saying unkind things about people. It made me laugh so much that I stopped being unkind and cross."

Later Martha went home to see her family. Mary felt very alone. She went out into the gardens and ran and ran. Then she began to feel better. The sunshine made everywhere look nicer. She went into the first kitchen garden and she found Ben Weatherstaff there. Ben seemed to be happier because of the sunshine, too. For the first time he spoke to her before she spoke to him.

"Spring's coming. Can you smell it?" he asked.

Mary thought she could. "I can smell something nice and fresh," she said.

"That's the spring in the earth," Ben said. "It's making things grow. Soon you'll see the little green points coming up out of the earth."

Soon she heard the robin. He, too, was very happy this morning. He walked about near Mary's feet.

"Do you remember me?" she asked him.

"Remember you!" cried Ben Weatherstaff almost crossly. "Of course he remembers you! He knows everything in this garden. He's never seen a little girl before, and he wants to know more about you."

"Are things growing in his garden?" Mary asked.

"What garden?" Ben asked angrily.

"The one where he lives. Are the flowers

there dead?" Mary wanted to know so much.

"Ask him," said Ben, and he looked down at the robin. "He's the only one who knows."

Ten years was a long time, Mary thought. She was born ten years ago. She thought that she liked the secret garden in the same way that she liked the robin and Dickon and Martha's mother. She went to walk by the wall where she had first seen the robin. And then – the most wonderful thing happened – all because of Ben Weatherstaff's robin.

He was standing near her on the earth by the wall. He had followed her. She was so pleased that she cried out: "You *do* remember me! You do! How wonderful!"

Then suddenly she saw something in the earth near the robin: it was a metal ring. She bent down to look at it. And it was not just a ring – there was a key, too. It looked very old.

Mary stood and looked at the key. "Perhaps it's the key to the secret garden," she thought. She stood there for a long time. If it really was the key to the secret garden, she would be able to go there whenever she liked – if she could find the door. Then nobody would know where she was. She liked this thought very much.

She walked up and down by the wall. It seemed so foolish, she thought, to be so near the garden, to have the key, and not to know where the door was. But she kept the key so that she would be ready if she found the door.

Chapter 9
The secret garden

The next morning Martha was back. She told Mary all about her day at home.

Then Mary went outside and into the part of the gardens where she had found the key. Then she saw the robin, and she laughed because she knew that he had followed her.

"You showed me the key yesterday," she said to him. "Perhaps you'll show me the door today, but I don't believe that you know where it is!"

When she was in India, she had heard a great deal about magic, and she always said that what happened next was magic. She was standing near the wall when suddenly the wind blew the plants to one side. She looked – and there in the wall was a door. Her heart beat noisily. She could not believe it! She found the key hole in the door and the key went in quite easily. She tried to turn it – it was difficult, but it did turn.

She looked behind her quickly, but there was no one near. Then she took a deep breath, opened the door, and went inside quickly. She shut the door behind her.

She could not believe it! She was standing inside the secret garden!

The garden was the strangest place Mary had ever seen. It was like a garden in a fairy story. There were high walls all around, and because it

Mary puts the key into the door of the secret garden

was winter, all the plants were brown and dead-looking. There was no green anywhere, and Mary did not know whether the garden was alive or dead. After ten years the trees had grown so much that they had made bridges over the spaces between each other.

"How quiet it is!" said Mary softly. Even the robin, who was sitting at the top of his tree, did not move. "And I am the first person who has spoken here for ten years!"

She walked around the garden with the robin, who wanted to show her everything. It was so quiet that she felt that she was a hundred miles away from anyone, and yet she did not feel alone. She had found a world of her own. As she walked around the garden, she noticed a lot of little green points which showed above the earth.

"They must be spring flowers," she thought. "The garden isn't quite dead." This made her feel happy.

Mary did not know anything about gardening, but the grass grew too closely around the little green points, so she pulled it up to give the flowers more space to grow. And this was how she passed her first morning in the secret garden. She was very busy. When it was time to go into the house to eat she could not believe that she had been working for three hours.

"I'll come back this afternoon," she said happily.

At lunch she ate so much that Martha was

pleased. They talked about plants and flowers during the meal, and Mary asked Martha questions about the things she had seen that morning. She was careful not to say which part of the garden she had been in.

After lunch Mary sat by the fire and said quietly: "I wish I had a little spade."

Martha laughed. "What do you want a spade for? Are you going to use it in the garden?"

"Yes, Martha. I'd like to make a little garden of my own. I'd like to plant seeds and watch flowers grow."

"Well!" said Martha. "My mother was right. She said that you should have a little garden of your own. She thought that it would make you happy."

"Your mother knows a lot of things, doesn't she?" said Mary. "I wonder how much a little spade costs?"

"Not much," Martha answered.

"I've got quite a lot of money," Mary said.

"I wonder ..." said Martha thoughtfully. "Yes, I know. We'll write to Dickon and ask him to buy you a spade and some seeds."

"But how will I get the things when Dickon buys them?"

"He'll bring them himself," said Martha.

"I will see him at last!" cried Mary. "I want to see him so much."

So together Martha and Mary wrote Dickon a letter.

Chapter 10
Dickon

The sun shone every day for the next week, and Mary often went to her secret garden. It was like a fairy garden, and she loved it. She liked being outside in the wind; she liked working around the little green points. It really was a secret garden – because no one knew where she was. She liked this thought most.

During that week, she and Ben Weatherstaff talked a great deal more. He almost seemed to like her now, and although he often sounded cross, she began to like him, too. He told her more about the plants and flowers that she had found in the secret garden. But again she was very careful not to tell him too much.

One day at the end of the week, Mary was playing near some trees in one of the kitchen gardens when she heard a strange, low sound. She wanted to know what it was, so she went nearer. And then she saw Dickon. As soon as she saw the boy, she knew that he must be Dickon.

He was standing under a tree, and all around him were little animals. He was playing a pipe very softly. None of the animals looked frightened even when Mary came towards him.

"I'm Dickon," he said, "and I know you are Mary."

He was about twelve years old, his nose turned up at the end, and he had very blue eyes. He had a wide mouth and he laughed a great deal. He was not a good-looking boy, but he was very friendly. He spoke to Mary as if he knew her well, and as if he liked her, too.

"I've brought your spade and your seeds," he said.

Mary had not met many boys in her life, and she did not quite know what to say to Dickon. At last she said: "Will you show me the seeds, please? Let's sit down and look at them."

"Well," said Dickon. "These are little white flowers which smell lovely. Then these are a beautiful deep red colour." Then he stopped and listened. "Where's that little robin who's singing to us?"

"He's in that tree," said Mary. "He's Ben Weatherstaff's robin, but he knows me, too."

"Yes, he does," said Dickon. "And he likes you."

"Do you understand everything that birds say?" Mary asked him. She could not believe that she was really talking to Dickon at last.

"Well," said Dickon. "I think I do, and they think I do. And that's what's important."

Dickon laughed, and then he talked a lot more about the seeds. He told her how to plant them. Suddenly he turned to her and said: "Tell me where your garden is. We can go and plant the seeds together."

Mary's face went red and then white and then red again. She did not know what to say. Dickon could not understand why she did not answer. At last she said: "Can you keep a secret?"

Dickon still did not understand, but he said: "Of course I can. I keep secrets all the time. I don't tell other boys where the animals and birds live, do I?"

"Listen," said Mary very quickly. "I've stolen a garden. No one owns it, and no one wants it. No one takes care of it – only me. I shall die if anyone takes it from me."

Dickon was surprised because Mary loved the garden so much. "Where is it?" he said quietly.

"Come with me, and I'll show you," she answered, and she led him into her secret garden.

"This is my secret garden," she said, when she had shut the door behind them, "and I am the only person in the whole world who wants it to be alive."

Chapter 11
Dickon sees the secret garden

Dickon stood and looked round and round the garden.

"Eh!" he said very softly. "It's a strange place. But it's very pretty. It's as if it were asleep."

Then he walked all round the garden as quietly and softly as Mary had done on her first morning there.

"I never thought that I'd see this place," he said at last.

"Did you know about it?" asked Mary.

"Ssssh! Speak quietly," said Dickon. "Someone might hear us. Yes, I knew about it. Martha told me."

"Will there be roses in the summer?" Mary asked. "Are the plants alive or dead? Can you tell?"

"They aren't all dead," said Dickon. And he took his knife and cut a piece off one of the rose trees. Although it looked dead on the outside there was a little green part inside. It was still alive. "There's a lot of dead wood here," he went on. "We ought to cut it away. But the tree is alive for sure."

"Oh, I'm so glad it's alive," said Mary. "Let's go round the garden to see which plants are still alive."

And together they went from tree to tree and plant to plant. Then Dickon showed Mary how to use the spade. They both worked very hard that morning. Suddenly Dickon noticed some of the places where Mary had moved the grass from around the little green points.

"Who did that?" he asked.

"I did," answered Mary.

"I thought you didn't know anything about gardening," he said.

"I don't," she said.

"Well, you did the right thing, Mary. You've done a lot of work, haven't you?"

"Yes," said Mary. "And it's making me strong. I don't feel tired any more, and I love the smell of the earth."

Then Dickon said, "But there's still a lot more work to do here."

"Will you help me to do it?" Mary asked him. "Please, Dickon, please."

"Of course I'll help you," he answered. "I'll come every day if you want me to. I want to make this garden alive again more than anything in the world. We'll have a lot of fun together."

He began to walk about thoughtfully. Then he said: "But I don't want this garden to look like the other big gardens. I don't want it to be too orderly, do you?"

"No," said Mary. "I don't. I like it the way it is now. If we make it too orderly, like other gardens, it won't be a secret any more." She

Mary and Dickon look at the plants in the garden

stopped and thought, and then she said: "Dickon, you're as nice as Martha said you were. I like you very much. I like five people now."

Dickon laughed. "Only five people?" he asked. "Who are the other four?"

"Your mother and Martha, and the robin and Ben Weatherstaff." Then she asked thoughtfully: "Do you like me?"

"Yes, I do," he answered. "And so does the robin. We both like you very much."

Then they worked again. Mary felt so happy; she remembered that first morning with Dickon for the rest of her life. It was time to go back to the house to eat too soon, and she had to leave Dickon. He had his food with him, so he stayed in the garden. Mary did not want to leave him. She was frightened that he might go away and never come back.

When she left, she said: "You will never tell anyone, will you?"

"Eh! No, Mary, I won't tell anyone. You're as safe in this garden as the animals and the birds are on the moor." And Dickon laughed. Mary knew that he was telling the truth.

Chapter 12
Mary meets Mr Craven

"I've seen Dickon!" Mary cried as soon as she saw Martha. "I've seen him!"

"And do you like him?" asked Martha.

"I think that he's ... wonderful!" said Mary.

She ate her meal quickly because she wanted to go back to Dickon, but Martha stopped her.

"Mary," she said. "Mr Craven has come back. He wants to see you."

Mary's face went white for the second time that day. "But why?" she asked. "He didn't want to see me when I first came to Misselthwaite. Why does he want to see me now?"

"Don't be frightened," said Martha. "He's going away again tomorrow, and he won't come back until next winter."

Then Mrs Medlock came in. She took Mary to see Mr Craven. Mary was very frightened. She knew that her uncle was not going to like her, and that she was not going to like him.

He was sitting in an armchair by the fire.

"Come here!" he said to her.

Mary went towards him, and she became the ugly, cross little girl from India. She looked at her uncle carefully. He was not really a hunchback, although he did not sit very straight. His face was very sad.

"Are you well?" he asked her.

"Yes," she answered.

"Do they take good care of you?"

"Yes."

"You are very thin," he went on.

"But I'm getting fatter," Mary answered. She wanted to say more, but she could not.

Then he asked her, "Are you happy? Do you want a teacher? Do you want anything?"

"Oh, please, I don't want a teacher yet," said Mary. "But there is one thing I'd like ... May I ... may I have a little piece of earth?"

"Earth?" her uncle said, surprised. "What do you mean?"

"To plant seeds in – to watch things grow – to make a garden," Mary answered. She was very frightened that he was going to say no.

Mr Craven looked very strange when she said this. He seemed to remember something. "A piece of earth," he said quietly. "Yes, of course you can have a piece of earth. Take as much as you want, and make it come alive." He looked very tired now, and said: "You must go now. I am very tired. I'm going away tomorrow. I won't be back until next winter."

As Mary walked back to her room, she thought: "He is really a nice man, but he looks so sad. Poor, Mr Craven."

When she got back to her own room, it was too late to go to the secret garden again that day. But she hoped that Dickon would come back the next day.

Chapter 13
"I am Colin"

During the night, however, it began to rain. Mary woke up and could not go to sleep again because she felt too cross. The wind was making a crying noise around the house, and the sound of it made her feel sad.

Then suddenly the noise changed. "It isn't the wind now," she said. "It's the crying that I heard before."

She got out of bed, took a candle and went out into the passage. She went to the place where she had seen Mrs Medlock on the day that she had opened doors. The noise was nearer. Someone was crying. She listened at the door. Yes, someone was crying in that room.

She opened the door quickly. Inside there was a bedroom with a large bed in it. A boy was lying on the bed, and he was crying. He did not seem to be in pain, but he sounded tired and cross. He was about ten years old, and he had a thin, white face. His eyes were very big and he did not look very healthy.

"Who are you?" the boy asked. He was frightened. "Are you real?"

"Of course I'm real," Mary answered. She was frightened, too. "Are you real?"

He looked at her hard. "Yes, I am. I'm Colin Craven. Who are you?"

Mary looked at him hard, too. "I'm Mary Lennox. Mr Craven is my uncle. I came to live here when my mother and father died."

"Mr Craven is my father," said the boy.

"No one told me that my uncle had a son," Mary said.

"Come here," the boy said. "You are real, aren't you? I often see people when I'm asleep. You might be one of them," and he touched her hand.

"Did no one tell you that I was here?" she said.

"No," he answered. "Because they thought it might make me ill. I don't want people to see me. I don't want people to talk about me."

"Why not?" asked Mary.

"Because I'm always ill. I'm going to be a hunchback if I live. But I shan't live."

"This is a very strange house," Mary said quietly. "Everything is a secret. Does your father come to see you?"

"Not often," answered Colin. "He doesn't want to see me. When he sees me, he thinks about my mother. She died when I was born. I think he hates me."

"He hates the garden because she died," Mary said thoughtfully.

"What garden?" the boy asked.

"Oh – just a garden that she used to like – that's all. Mr Craven shut the garden when his wife died, and he hid the key. No one has been into the garden for ten years."

But Colin wanted to know more about the garden. He asked her to tell him about it. Where was it? Had she looked for the door? Had she asked the gardeners about it? When Mary told him that no one would talk about it, he said something which frightened her very much.

"I could make them talk about it," he said. "All the servants must do what I want. If I live, Misselthwaite Manor will be mine one day, and they know that."

Mary was sad because Colin did not seem to want to live. But at that minute, she was more frightened that he would tell everyone about the secret garden.

"I want the servants to find the key, and to open the door," he went on. "I want them to take me there in my wheelchair." For the first time in his life Colin was interested in something.

"Oh, please ... don't ... don't do that!" Mary cried.

"Why not?" he asked. He did not understand. "I thought you wanted to see it."

"I do," she answered, "but if you make them open the door, it will never be a secret again."

But Colin still did not understand. "A secret?" he asked. "What do you mean?"

So Mary tried to tell him. "You see," she said, "if we can find the garden, it will be our own garden. Only we will know about it. Don't you see? It will be much more fun if it's a secret."

Mary and Colin in Colin's bedroom

At last Colin began to understand. "I've never had a secret before, but I think that secrets are nice."

Mary went on: "Perhaps we can find a boy to push your wheelchair, and then we can go to the garden alone. No one will know where we are. Then it will always be a secret garden. And you can come outside in the wind and the sunshine, and you will get better."

Then she said: "Will Mrs Medlock be very angry if she finds me here?"

"She will do what I tell her to do," said Colin. "I'm glad that you came tonight, and that's the only thing that's important."

"And I'm glad I came," said Mary.

"But I want you to be a secret, too," said Colin. "I shan't tell them about you. I'll only tell Martha. She will tell you when I want to see you. She often takes care of me."

"So Martha knew about you all the time?" Mary asked. Now she understood why Martha had looked so frightened when she had heard Colin before.

They talked for a long time. At last Mary said, "I've been with you a long time. You must sleep now. I'll sing to you and then perhaps you'll go to sleep. My servant in India used to sing this song to me."

Mary began to sing very softly. Soon Colin went to sleep, and Mary went back to her own room.

Chapter 14
Martha is frightened

It was still raining next morning. Mary could not go outside. When Martha came in, Mary told her: "I know who was crying."

A look of great fear went across Martha's face.

"Oh no!" she cried. "How?"

"I heard the noise again in the night," said Mary. "And I went to see what it was. It was Colin. I found him."

"Oh Mary," said Martha. "What have you done? I didn't tell you anything, but now they'll send me away. What shall I do?"

"They won't send you away, Martha," said Mary. "He liked me. We talked for a long time. He was glad that I came."

"Was he?" asked Martha. "Are you sure?" She did not believe Mary. "Did he let you look at him?"

"Yes. I looked at him all the time," Mary answered. "I think he liked me."

"I can't believe it. It must be magic," Martha said quietly.

"He wants me to talk to him every day," Mary went on. "He's not going to tell Mrs Medlock. It's a secret. He'll tell you when he wants to see me. Then you can tell me." She stopped. "What's wrong with him?" she asked.

"No one really knows," said Martha. "After his wife's death Mr Craven didn't want to see the baby. He thought that the child was going to be a hunchback. He almost wanted the child to die."

"But Colin isn't a hunchback," said Mary. "He didn't look like one."

"No, he isn't yet," said Martha. "But his father is frightened because his back is weak. Colin knows this. An important doctor came from London once. He saw Colin, and said that he wasn't a hunchback, and he wasn't going to be one. He said that the boy must go out in the fresh air. But Colin didn't believe him."

"I wonder," said Mary. "I got better when I went outside and watched flowers and plants growing. Do you think that Colin would get better, too?"

"I don't know. He says that he hates the garden and the wind. He had his worst illness when they took him into the rose garden. He thinks that he's going to die. He only sits in bed and reads books."

That afternoon Martha told Mary that Colin wanted to see her.

"It's magic," she said. "He has got up out of bed, and he's sitting in an armchair."

Mary went quickly. She did not want to see Colin as much as she wanted to see Dickon, but she wanted to see him very much.

In daylight Colin's room was very beautiful. It

was warm and pleasant.

"Come in," said Colin. "I've been thinking about you all morning."

"I've been thinking about you, too," said Mary. "Poor Martha, she's very frightened. She thinks that they will send her away. But she didn't tell me about you. I found you by myself."

"Tell Martha to come here," Colin said.

When Martha came in, he said: "You have to do what I want, don't you?"

"Yes, Colin," Martha answered.

"You are not to be frightened that they will send you away. If you do what I want, I will take care of you. That is all."

Martha went out. She looked very surprised. Mary looked thoughtful.

"What are you thinking about?" Colin asked her.

"I'm thinking about two things. Firstly, that you are like an Indian prince that I once saw. He spoke to his people in the same way that you speak to Martha. Everybody had to do what he wanted. He wasn't very nice."

"And what was the second thing?" Colin asked.

"I was thinking about you and Dickon. You are not at all like him."

"Who is Dickon?" he asked.

Mary wanted to talk about Dickon. "He's Martha's brother. He's twelve years old, and there is no one in the world like him. He can talk to every animal and bird. He plays a pipe very softly and they come to listen. He has lived on the moor all his life, and he knows where all the animals and birds live."

"I never see anything because I'm ill," said Colin sadly. "I can't go on the moor."

"Why not?" asked Mary. "You might go one day."

"No, I won't. I'm going to die. Everyone wants me to die."

"Don't be foolish. Who wants you to die?" Mary asked.

"The servants and Dr Craven. He's my father's brother. If I die, he'll get Misselthwaite Manor. I think that my father wants me to die, too."

"Oh no, he doesn't," said Mary. This talk of death made her feel sad. "Don't let's talk about death," she said. "Let's talk about life. Let's talk about Dickon."

They talked about Dickon and his mother and their little house on the moor. They talked about the little green points in the garden, and about Ben Weatherstaff's robin. They laughed about everything, and Colin felt happy. He did not remember that his back was weak.

Suddenly, Dr Craven and Mrs Medlock walked into the room. Dr Craven looked very frightened when he saw Mary.

"What's this?" he cried. "Are you all right, Colin? Are you all right?"

"Of course I'm all right," said Colin, and he spoke like the Indian prince again. "This is Mary Lennox. I asked her to come. I like her. I want to see her often. No one told her about me," he went on, because Mrs Medlock looked cross and frightened at the same time. "She heard me one night when I was crying, and she found me by herself."

Dr Craven told Colin he must remember that he was ill. Then he and Mrs Medlock went away.

"But I don't want to remember that I'm ill." Colin said to Mary as soon as they had gone. "I don't remember when I'm with you. That is why I like you, Mary. Now we'll have tea together and you can tell me more about India."

During the next week, Mary saw Colin every day. The week went very quickly, and the two children had a great deal of fun together. There was only one thing which Mary had to remember. She wanted to tell Colin that she had been inside the secret garden, but she did not know whether he could keep the secret. By the end of the week, however, Mary was sure that Colin would get better if he went outside. She knew that he did not want anyone to see him, but at last she asked him: "Would you be angry if Dickon saw you?"

"No, I don't think so," he answered. "Dickon is the one person in the world who wouldn't make me angry."

Chapter 15
The secret garden again

The next day Mary woke up very early. After a week of rain, the sky was blue again, and the sun was shining.

"It's warm," cried Mary. "The garden will begin to grow again. Oh, how wonderful!" She got out of bed and opened the window. "I must see the secret garden now!" she cried. "I can't wait!"

She dressed quickly and ran out into the gardens.

"I'm sure that Dickon will come today," she thought, and she ran even faster towards the secret garden.

But Dickon was in the garden before her. She saw him when she opened the door. He was working hard, and some of his animals were with him.

"Dickon!" Mary cried. "How did you get here so early? The sun has only just got up!"

Dickon laughed. "Eh!" he said, "I got up before the sun did. I couldn't stay in bed."

"Oh Dickon," Mary said. "I'm so happy."

They looked at all the new plants together. The green points had become flowers at last, and the roses were alive. Later in the summer there would be flowers on them. Even the plants which grew on the walls were becoming green.

"Everything is alive again," Mary said.

Suddenly Dickon stood quite still. He had seen the robin's red feathers. The little bird had just flown into a big tree.

"Keep still," Dickon told Mary. "He's working hard. He has found a wife and he's making a home for her where she can lay her eggs. We mustn't frighten him while he's building it. If we do, he'll never be our friend again."

So Mary and Dickon sat on the grass. Dickon spoke to Mary very softly. He told her not to watch the robin because that would frighten him.

"We mustn't talk about him, then," said Mary, "or I will watch him. There is something I want to ask you, Dickon. Do you know about Colin?"

Dickon turned to her and said, "Why? What do you know about him?"

"I've seen him," she answered. "He likes me. He says that when he is with me he doesn't remember that he's going to die."

"Well," said Dickon. "I'm glad that you know about him. I knew about him, but I had to hide it from you. I don't like hiding things."

"How do you know about Colin?" Mary asked him.

"Everyone knows that Mr Craven has a son," he answered. "But no one ever sees him, because he's a hunchback. Mr Craven can't look at the boy because he's so like his mother. Poor Mr Craven, he wishes that the child had never been born."

"He isn't a hunchback," said Mary. "But he thinks that he's going to be one. It's very sad. I've been thinking, Dickon," she went on. "Do you think that Colin could keep our secret?"

"I think so," said Dickon. "If he could, we could bring him out into the garden in his wheelchair. I'm sure that he would get better in the fresh air."

"The doctor from London said that he would," said Mary.

"Well, we must bring him out here as soon as possible," said Dickon.

Mary and Dickon worked very hard that morning. Mary went into the house for a meal, but she went out to the garden again quickly.

"Tell Colin that I can't come yet," she said to Martha. "I'm very busy in the garden. Dickon is waiting for me."

"Colin will be cross," answered Martha, but Mary did not listen.

Chapter 16
Mary and Colin quarrel

Mary did not go back to the house until the evening. Then she wanted to tell Colin about Dickon and his animals. But when she saw Martha, she knew that something was not right.

"Colin is very angry because you didn't go to see him," Martha told her.

Mary began to feel cross. The secret garden and Dickon were the two most important things in her life. Colin was fun sometimes, but he was not as important as the garden or Dickon.

She went to see him, however. He was in bed this time.

"Why didn't you come?" he asked her. He spoke like the Indian prince.

"Because I was working in the gardens with Dickon," she answered.

Colin looked cross. "I won't let that boy come here again," he said angrily.

This made Mary very cross. "If you send Dickon away, I'll never come into this room again," she shouted.

"You'll have to come if I want you to," cried Colin.

"I won't," she answered.

"Yes, you will," shouted Colin.

"No, I won't," Mary shouted.

And they shouted at each other for some

time. They said some very unkind things. At last Colin shouted: "Get out of this room!"

And Mary answered: "I'm going, and I won't come back! I wanted to tell you about Dickon and his animals, but I won't now."

She ran out of the room. She felt very angry, but also rather sad. Now she would never tell Colin her great secret.

When she got back to her room, she found some books on the table. They were presents from Mr Craven. There were some picture books, and two books about gardening.

"How kind he is," she thought, and then she began to think about Colin. She began to feel a little bit sorry for him. "Poor Colin," she thought. "Perhaps he has been thinking about his hunchback all afternoon. Perhaps I will go and see him tomorrow."

She went to bed early because she was tired, but she woke up suddenly during the night. There was a great noise. People were running along the passages, and far away someone was crying.

"It's Colin," she thought. "I don't know what to do, but someone must stop him."

Suddenly Martha came into her room. "Oh, Mary," she cried. "Please stop him! He'll hurt himself. Please stop him! He likes you."

So Mary went to Colin's room. When she saw him, she shouted: "Stop it! Stop it! Stop it! If you cry again, I'll cry too, and I can make more

51

noise than you can. I'll frighten you!"

Colin was so surprised that he almost stopped crying. No one had ever shouted at him before.

"I can't stop!" he cried. "I can't!"

"Yes, you can," Mary answered.

"I'm going to be a hunchback," he cried. "I know it! I felt my back, and it has changed."

"No, it hasn't. Don't be foolish," Mary said. "Let me see."

She looked at his back. It was very thin and weak, but it was quite straight, and she told him so.

"Of course you're not going to be a hunchback," she said loudly. "Your back is as good as mine."

Colin smiled weakly. He believed that Mary was telling the truth. "Do you think that I will live?" he asked her.

"Of course you'll live," she said. "But you'll have to go outside in the fresh air a great deal."

"I'll come with you," he said quietly.

"Now," said Mary, "you must go to sleep. Shall I sing to you again?"

"Will you tell me about the secret garden instead?" he asked her. "Have you found the key?"

"Yes, I think so," answered Mary. "I'll tell you about it tomorrow. Now go to sleep."

She held his hand, and sang very softly. He went to sleep very quickly.

Chapter 17
Mary tells Colin the secret

The next morning Mary slept late, because she was very tired. When Martha came in, she said: "Colin wants you to go to him as soon as you can. He seems to like you very much. I don't know why, because you were very angry with him last night." And she laughed. "He said, 'Please ask Mary to come.' I don't think he has ever said 'please' to anyone in his life before!"

Mary wanted very much to go to the secret garden, but she went to see Colin first.

"I'm glad you came," Colin said. "I feel very tired this morning. My whole body hurts. What are we going to do today?"

"Well," said Mary slowly. "First, I'm going to see Dickon, but I'll come back soon," she added quickly, because Colin looked so sad. "And when I come back, I'll tell you something very important – it's about the secret garden."

"Oh, how wonderful!" cried Colin. "Please come back quickly."

Mary went out into the garden, and Dickon was there before her again.

Every day now there were more things alive in the garden. It was like magic. Mary and Dickon sat down, and she told him what had happened during the night. Then she told him that Colin wanted to see him and his animals.

Dickon thought that this was a good plan, and he said he would come the next day.

The garden was so beautiful that Mary did not want to go back to Colin, but she did. And Colin looked very pleased to see her again.

She sat down and they talked about Dickon and his animals.

"Do they really understand what Dickon says?" asked Colin. "And does he really know what they say to him?"

"He says he does," Mary answered. "He says that anyone can understand an animal, although they must be one of the animal's friends."

"I wish I had friends," said Colin sadly. "But I don't like people, and people don't like me."

"Don't you like me?" Mary asked him.

"Yes," he said, and he sounded surprised.

"Ben Weatherstaff once told me that I was like him." Mary said. "He said, 'We don't look nice and friendly, and I don't think that we are!' Perhaps you are the same. But," she stopped to think, "I think that I am nicer now that I know the robin and Dickon."

"Mary," said Colin quietly, "I'm sorry that I said those unkind things about Dickon yesterday. I hated him because you liked him, but I made a mistake. I do want to see him very much."

"I'm glad that you said that," Mary answered, "because ... because ..." she stopped. "Can you keep a secret? Can you really keep a secret?"

"Yes, yes," Colin cried.

"Well," said Mary, "Dickon will come to see you tomorrow and he'll bring his animals with him." Colin's eyes grew bigger and bigger. "But that isn't everything," she said. "Listen. This is better. There is a door to the secret garden, and I have found the key."

Colin could not believe it. "Will I see it?" he cried.

"Of course you'll see it," Mary answered. And then she told him what the garden was really like.

Later that day Dr Craven came to see Colin. Mrs Medlock had told him what had happened during the night, so he was very surprised that Colin was not in bed.

"I'm sorry that you were ill last night, Colin," he said.

"I'm much better now," Colin answered. Again Mary thought of the Indian prince. "I want to go outside," he went on. "I want some fresh air."

"You must be very careful," said Dr Craven. "I thought that you didn't like fresh air."

"I don't when I'm alone," Colin answered. "But Mary is going to come with me. Dickon is going to push my wheelchair. We will go alone."

Dr Craven did not like this plan. He thought that it might make Colin ill again, but he could not stop the boy. He left the room, and he could not believe what he had seen.

Chapter 18
Colin sees the secret garden at last

They had to wait for a week, however, before Colin could go to the garden, because there were some very windy days, and then he caught a cold. But Dickon went to see Colin every day and told him what was happening outside.

At last Colin was outside. Dickon pushed the wheelchair, and Mary walked beside it. Colin looked up at the sky, and breathed the fresh air. His eyes grew bigger and bigger.

They saw no one in the gardens, but they walked around for a long time before they went into the secret garden.

"This is where the robin showed me the key," Mary said. "And this – this is the door. Push the wheelchair inside quickly, Dickon!" she cried.

Colin covered his eyes with his hands. He did not look until they were inside the garden. Then he looked at everything, in the same way that Mary and Dickon had done when they first saw the garden.

"I will get better!" he cried. "Mary and Dickon, I will get well! I will live for ever and ever!"

That afternoon Colin felt that the whole world was good and beautiful. He began to feel better and to look better. His face became less white, and he laughed all the time. He sat in his wheelchair under one of the fruit trees while Dickon and Mary worked. They brought him things to see. Then Dickon pushed the chair slowly around the garden, and they stopped and looked at all the wonderful things. Colin thought that the garden was like a fairy garden.

"I wonder if we will see the robin?" he asked Dickon. Then he noticed an old tree. "Why is part of that tree broken?" he asked.

"It happened a long time ago," Dickon answered. He stopped, and then he said suddenly: "Look, look, there's the robin."

So Colin saw the robin at last, and he forgot to ask about the broken tree. Mary and Dickon were very glad about this, because the broken tree had caused the death of his mother, and they did not want to tell him that.

"I don't want this afternoon to end," said Colin slowly. "But I'll come back tomorrow, and the day after and the day after that. I've seen the spring and now I want to see the summer. I want to grow with the garden."

"And you will," said Dickon. "You'll soon be able to walk and work and use a spade like Mary and me."

"Walk!" said Colin, very surprised. "Use a spade! Will I?"

"Of course," said Mary and Dickon together. "You've got legs, haven't you? We must make them strong."

It was nearly evening, and the sun was going

down. The garden was very still and quiet.

Suddenly Colin said, "Who is that man?"

"Which man?" cried Mary and Dickon.

Colin pointed to the wall. Mary and Dickon turned, and there was Ben Weatherstaff. They could only see his head over the top of the wall. He looked very angry. From the place he had climbed to he could only see Mary.

"What are you doing, you bad girl?" he shouted. "How did you get into that garden?"

"The robin showed me the way," Mary answered.

Dickon pushed Colin's wheelchair nearer Ben Weatherstaff, and when Ben saw Colin he looked and looked.

"Do you know who I am?" Colin asked him.

"Yes, I do," answered Ben, "because you look so like your mother. How did you get here? I thought you were a hunchback."

"I'm not a hunchback," said Colin loudly. "I'm not!"

"No, he's not!" Mary shouted too. "I've seen his back and he's not a hunchback."

"Come here!" Colin shouted to Dickon. "Come here at once!" And he started to stand up. Mary's face went white, because she was very frightened. She said quietly again and again. "He can do it! He can do it!" And Colin did. He held Dickon's arm; he put his thin legs on the ground; and suddenly he was standing up, with his head held high.

"Now – look at me, Ben Weatherstaff!" he shouted. "Am I a hunchback?"

"No, no!" Ben answered, and Mary thought that she saw tears in the old man's eyes. "No – I can't believe it! Eh! People haven't told the truth about you, my boy. God bless you!"

Colin said, "Come here. Mary will show you the way. I want to talk to you. Be quick!"

Before Ben Weatherstaff came into the garden with Mary, Colin said to Dickon: "I can stand and now I'm going to walk to that tree. I will stand against it when Ben Weatherstaff comes."

He walked over to the tree.

When Ben came through the door, he could not believe what he saw.

"What work do you do in the gardens?" Colin asked him.

"Everything," Ben answered. "They give me work because your mother liked me, although I'm really too old now. This was her garden and she loved it."

"It's my garden now, and I love it, too," said Colin. "But it's a secret. No one must know about it – only Mary, Dickon, you and me."

Just then Colin noticed Mary's spade on the ground. He picked it up, and he began to work with it. He did not work very well, but he looked very happy.

"And now," he said, as he put the spade down, "I've walked and I've used a spade. You said that I would, Dickon, and I've done it!"

59

Chapter 19
Magic

Dr Craven was waiting for them when they got back to the house.

"You have stayed outside too long," he said to Colin. "You must be more careful."

"But I'm not tired," answered Colin, "I feel better, and tomorrow I shall stay outside all day."

Dr Craven did not look pleased about this, but he knew that he could not stop Colin.

After he had gone, Mary said to Colin: "I feel sorry for Dr Craven."

"Why?" asked Colin. "Because he won't get Misselthwaite Manor?"

"No," answered Mary. "Because he must be nice to you, although you are unkind to him."

"Am I unkind?" asked Colin.

"Yes, you are," answered Mary. She was not being unkind herself; she wanted to tell Colin the truth. "No one has ever done anything that you didn't like because you were always ill."

"But I'm not ill now. I'm going to get better," he said. "And I'm not going to be unkind again."

"Good," said Mary. "The garden and its magic will help you, because there is magic in the garden."

During the next few months there really was magic in the garden. The children went there every day, and as Colin grew stronger, the garden grew more and more beautiful. There were flowers everywhere, and the roses were wonderful. Colin watched each change carefully, and Dickon told him and Mary about the plants and flowers and the animals and the birds. Each day Colin worked and walked more. This was the real magic of the garden. It made Colin want to get better, and he did. One day he walked all around the garden. Mary and Dickon walked on each side of him; Ben Weatherstaff walked behind them and all Dickon's animals came at the end. They walked very slowly, and they stopped often, but Colin was very happy. "The magic is making me strong!" he cried. "The magic is in me!"

When he was back in his wheelchair under the tree he said: "I'm not going to tell Dr Craven that I'm better. This is to be the greatest secret of all. I'm not going to tell anyone until I can run and walk like Dickon. I shall come here every day in my wheelchair. Then, when my father comes home, I shall walk into his room and say: 'Here I am. I'm very well and I'm going to live to be a man. The magic of the garden has helped me.' "

"He won't believe you," Mary said, and she laughed. "He'll think that he's asleep!"

There was one thing which was difficult for Colin now. He was hungry all the time. He was frightened that the servants might learn about his secret because he ate so much. It was strange that a sick boy could eat so much! Colin and his

Mary, Colin, Dickon and Ben walk around the secret garden

friends did not know what to do. But then Dickon told his mother, and she had a plan. Every day she gave Dickon fresh bread for Mary and Colin. After that Colin did not want to eat so much at meal times.

Poor Dr Craven! He did not know what to think. Before Colin went out into the gardens every day he ate nothing. Then, when he first went out, he ate much more. But now suddenly he did not eat again. It was very strange! But there was something even more strange – although Colin was not eating again, he was still growing fatter.

But no one learnt what the secret was. Colin told no one where they went, although Dr Craven often asked him. The three children were outside all day when it wasn't raining. Colin grew stronger and fatter all the time.

One day Colin said to Mary: "I wish my father would come home. I want to tell him the secret myself, but I think that the servants are going to learn about it soon. I'm getting quite fat, and I don't look the same. I wish that the magic would bring my father home."

Chapter 20
Mary and Colin meet Dickon's mother

One day, after it had rained for a week, Mary, Colin and Dickon were in the garden again, working hard, when suddenly Colin stopped.

"Mary, Dickon!" he cried. "Look at me! I'm really well at last! It's real. I'm well!" He had thought about it for such a long time, and now it was true. He felt very happy. "I will live for ever and ever!" he shouted. "Because the magic has helped me!"

Just then he looked towards the door of the garden.

"Who is that?" he asked. "Who is it?"

A woman was standing by the door. She had a very kind face, and she was laughing. Dickon ran across the grass. "It's mother!" he shouted, and Mary and Colin ran, too.

"I knew that you wanted to see her," said Dickon, "and so I told her where to find the door."

Colin was very happy. "I've always wanted to see you, Mrs Sowerby," he told her. "Even when I was ill. You and Dickon and the garden were the first things that I wanted to see in my whole life."

Mrs Sowerby did not say anything. She just looked kindly at the three young faces around her.

"Are you surprised that I'm so well?" Colin asked her next.

"Yes, I am," she answered. "And I'm also surprised because you look so like your mother."

"Do you think my father will like me?" Colin asked her. He was very frightened that his father would not want to see him. He had seen his father so little in his life that he thought his father did not like him.

"I'm sure he will, Colin," she answered.

Ben Weatherstaff came into the garden just then.

"Well, Mrs Sowerby," he said. "What do you think of Colin? Hasn't he grown strong? I can't believe that two months ago his legs were so thin that he couldn't walk."

"I think he's wonderful," Dickon's mother said, and then she turned to Mary. "And you've grown strong and healthy, too, Mary. You're a pretty girl now. I'm sure that you're like your mother, too."

Then they showed Mrs Sowerby everything in the garden – every tree and plant that had come alive. Mary and Colin liked her very much. She was so kind and quiet.

At last Colin asked her: "Do you believe in magic?"

"Yes, I do," she answered. "There are many names for it, but I know what you mean."

Colin and Mary were very pleased when they heard this.

Mrs Sowerby had brought a basket of food with her. After they had walked around the garden, they sat down under one of the fruit trees. They ate a great deal, and while they ate Mrs Sowerby told them many stories about her children, and the moor and Yorkshire. They laughed a great deal.

"Ssshhh!" said Colin. "We mustn't make so much noise – someone might hear us. Oh, Mrs Sowerby, it's so difficult. When we're together we want to laugh all the time, and we mustn't." Then he said quietly: "Do you think that my father will come home soon?"

"Yes. He'll come home soon," she answered. "He must come home. He'll be very happy when he sees you, Colin."

Then they talked about other things. They made plans for a visit to Mrs Sowerby's house. And then, too soon, it was time for her to go, and for Colin and Mary to go back to the house. Before Dickon's mother left, Colin went and stood in front of her, and said: "I wish you were my mother as well as Dickon's."

Her face looked almost sad when he said this. She put her arms round him and said: "Dear Colin! Your father must come home soon! He must!"

Chapter 21
In the garden

While Mary was at Misselthwaite Manor, she learnt something very important. She learnt not to think only about herself. Now she thought a great deal about Dickon and his animals, about the secret garden and about Colin. She probably did not know that she had changed, but after six months she was a much nicer child.

Colin changed in the same way. Before he met Mary, he had thought only about himself – about his illnesses, his hunchback, and his sadness. But when he met Mary and Dickon and visited the secret garden every day, he began to change.

While these changes were happening at Misselthwaite Manor, Colin's father was travelling in countries far away from England. He visited Sweden, Norway, Switzerland and Italy. He never stayed in one place for long, and he was always very sad. He thought only about his dead wife, his sick son, and his own sadness.

One day at the end of summer, he was in Italy. He was sitting in a quiet garden and he fell asleep. While he slept, he remembered his wife. He thought he could hear her calling to him.

"Where are you, my dear?" he asked.

"I'm in the garden – in the garden," she answered.

Soon after, he woke up, and later he walked back to the house where he was staying. There was a letter for him. He opened it, and this is what it said:

Dear Mr Craven,

I hope that you will not be angry because I have written to you. You must come home to Misselthwaite Manor. Please Mr Craven, it is very important. Please come back as soon as possible.

Yours sincerely,
Susan Sowerby.

Mr Craven read the letter twice. "I will go back to Misselthwaite. I'll go now," he said.

A few days later he was back in Yorkshire. He began to feel happier, but he did not know why. During the journey he thought a great deal about Colin and about Mrs Sowerby's letter. He wondered why she had written to him. He did not know her very well, but he knew that she was a kind woman and a good mother. What was so important? Then he remembered what his wife had said while he was sleeping in the quiet garden in Italy.

As soon as he reached Misselthwaite Manor, he saw Mrs Medlock. His first question was: "How is Colin, Mrs Medlock?"

"Well, Mr Craven," she answered slowly, "he's ... he's not the same."

"Is he still sick?" Mr Craven asked.

"Well ... we don't know," Mrs Medlock answered.

"Why not?"

"Well ... he's getting fatter, but he doesn't eat anything. He seems to be happier, and he even laughs with Mary Lennox and Dickon Sowerby. But he's the same as ever with Dr Craven and me."

"Where is he now?" Mr Craven asked.

"In the garden," Mrs Medlock answered.

"In the garden!" Mr Craven cried. "In the garden!" Those were the words that his wife had said to him in his sleep.

He went out into the gardens. He walked slowly, because he was thinking about the ten years since his wife's death. He wondered why he was going back to her garden after so many years. When he got to the place where he had hidden the key, he stopped.

"How strange," he thought. "I can hear children's voices, and yet no one has been inside this garden for ten years."

The sounds grew clearer. They were laughing. Suddenly a boy came through the door. He was running so fast that he almost made Mr Craven fall over. He was a tall, good-looking boy with dark hair and big eyes. Mr Craven knew at once who he was.

"Who? ... What? ... Who?" he cried.

Mary was standing near Colin, and she heard him say: "Father, I'm Colin. Can you believe it?"

Mr Craven could only say quietly: "In the garden! In the garden!"

"Yes," said Colin. "I'm better because of the garden. The garden and Mary and Dickon and his animals – and the magic – made me better. No one knows I am better. It has been a secret. I wanted you to know first."

Mr Craven was so happy that he could not speak.

"Aren't you glad, father?" Colin asked him. "Aren't you glad? I'm going to live for ever and ever!"

The garden was very beautiful in the late summer. Mr Craven looked at everything.

"I thought it would be dead," he said.

"So did Mary," said Colin. "But it has come alive!"

They all sat under a tree, and Colin told the story of the secret garden. They laughed happily about the robin, and Ben Weatherstaff, and the garden and the secret.

At last Colin said: "It will not be a secret any more. The servants will be very frightened when they see me, but I am never going to sit in that wheelchair again. I will walk back to the house with you, father."

And he did. All the servants were watching as Mr Craven and his son walked back to the house together. Colin looked very happy and so did his father, and Colin looked as healthy as any boy in Yorkshire.

Questions

Questions on each chapter

1 1 Who took care of Mary in India?
  2 What happened to her father and mother?
  3 Why did no one care about Mary? (Because . . .)

2 1 Who was Mary's uncle?
  2 Who met Mary in London?
  3 What was the matter with Mr Craven?
   (He was . . ., and his wife . . .)

3 1 What do you call high land in Yorkshire where only rough
   grass grows?
  2 When is the moor pretty?

4 1 Why couldn't Mary dress herself? (Because . . .)
  2 Who was Dickon?
  3 What did Mr Craven do with the key of the locked garden?

5 1 Where was the robin when Mary first saw it?
  2 How did Ben Weatherstaff call the robin to him?
  3 When did Mary sound like a "real child"?

6 1 What made Mary hungry?
  2 What happened to Mrs Craven in the garden?
  3 What sound did Mary hear inside the house?

7 1 How many rooms were there in the house?
  2 What did Mrs Medlock do to Mary?

8 1 What was the nice fresh smell?
  2 What did Mary see near the robin?
  3 Why did she keep it?

9 1 Why hadn't Mary seen the door before?
(Because plants . . .)
  2 What work did Mary do in the garden?
  3 What did Mary and Martha write?

10 1 What did Dickon bring?
  2 What secret did Dickon keep all the time?

11 1 Dickon already knew about the secret garden. Who had
told him?
  2 Mary now liked five people. Who were they?

12 1 What did Mary ask Mr Craven for?
  2 What was his answer?

13 1 What was Colin's full name?
  2 Why didn't Colin's father want to see him?
  3 How did Mary send Colin to sleep?

14 1 What did the doctor from London say about Colin?
  2 How did Colin speak to Martha? (Like . . .)
  3 What will Dr Craven get if Colin dies?

15 1 What was the robin doing?
  2 What did people believe about Colin's back?

16 1 Why did Colin and Martha quarrel?
  2 What did Mary tell Colin about his back?

17 1 Who was coming to see Colin the next day?
  2 What surprised Dr Craven when he saw Colin?

18 1 Why didn't Mary and Dickon want to talk about the broken
tree? (Because . . .)
  2 Why did Colin stand against a tree?
  3 Who must know about the secret garden? (Only . . .)

19 1 What was Dickon's mother's plan? (Every day . . .)
  2 What was the result? (Colin didn't . . .)

20 1 What had happened to Colin in the secret garden?
(He had grown . . .)
  2 What had happened to Mary?

21 1 What had Mary learned?
  2 Where was Colin's father when the letter arrived?
  3 Who ran out of the garden?

Questions on the whole story

These are harder questions. Read the Introduction and think hard about the questions before you answer them. Some of them ask for your opinion, and there is no fixed answer.

1 *Mary* was "not at all a nice child" in India. Can you finish these sentences?
  a Perhaps that was because her mother . . .
  b Perhaps it was because the servants . . .

2 Martha:
  a How did she show kindness to Mary?
  b What did Mary learn from her about the moor, and about outdoor life?
  c Who were Martha's favourite people?

3 Dickon:
  a He loved animals, and they loved him. Can you give examples?
  b What did he teach Mary?

4 Mrs Sowerby:
  a What did Mary know about her before she met her?
  b Why did she write to Mr Craven?

5 Colin:
  a At first he was like Mary in some ways. What were they?
  b Why was he so unhappy? Can you finish these sentences?
    1 Because his father . . .
    2 Because he thought . . .
    3 Because no one . . .
  c What do you think was really the "magic" that made him well?

6 Mr Craven:
  a What is the "happy ending" to the story for him?
  b Why was he so unhappy before that?
  c Is it right for him to have a happy ending? Why?

New words

hunchback
a person with a bent backbone

important
mattering a lot; **it isn't important** = it doesn't matter

interested
wanting to know about (something)

lamb
a baby sheep

moor
high land where only rough grass grows

novel
a long story that fills a whole book

robin
a small bird with red feathers on the front of its body

secret
known by only a few people

spade
an instrument for digging a garden